SPECIAL OFFERS FOR MR MEN AND LITTLE MISS READERS

In every Mr Men and Li cial token.
Collect only six tokens and of your choice
featuring all your f ends.

And for the first 4,000 nd you a
Mr Men activity pad* and a bookmark* as well – absolutely free!

Return this page with six tokens from Mr Men and/or Little Miss books to:
Marketing Department, World International Publishing, Egmont House,
PO Box 111, 61 Great Ducie Street, Manchester M60 3BL.

Your name:_____

Address:_____

_____

_____ Postcode: _____

Signature of parent or guardian: _____

I enclose **six** tokens – please send me a Mr Men poster ☐

I enclose **six** tokens – please send me a Little Miss poster ☐

We may occasionally wish to advise you of other children's books that
we publish. If you would rather we didn't, please tick this box ☐

*while stocks last   (Please note: this offer is limited to a maximum of two posters per household.)

Collect six of these tokens.
You will find one inside every
Mr Men and Little Miss book
which has this special offer.

1
TOKEN

Please remove this page carefully

JOIN THE MR MEN & LITTLE MISS CLUB

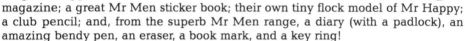

Treat your child to membership of the long-awaited Mr Men & Little Miss Club and see their delight when they receive a personal letter from Mr Happy and Little Miss Giggles together with a great value Welcome Pack.

In the Pack they'll discover a unique collection of items for learning and fun: their own personal membership card; a club badge **with their name on**; an exclusive club members' cassette tape with two Mr Men stories and four songs; a copy of the excellent Fun To Learn™ Mr Men magazine; a great Mr Men sticker book; their own tiny flock model of Mr Happy; a club pencil; and, from the superb Mr Men range, a diary (with a padlock), an amazing bendy pen, an eraser, a book mark, and a key ring!

And that's not all. On their birthday and again at Christmas they'll get a card from the Mr Men and Little Misses. And every month the Mr Men magazine (available from newsagents) features exclusive offers for club members.

If all this could be bought in the shops you would expect to pay at least £12.00. But a year's membership is superb value at just **£7.99** (plus 70p postage). To enrol your child please send **your** name, address and telephone number together with **your child's** full name, date of birth and address (including postcode) and a cheque or postal order for £8.69 (payable to Mr Men & Little Miss Club) to: Mr Happy, Happyland (Dept. WI), PO Box 142, Horsham RH13 5FJ. Or call 01403 242727 to pay by credit card.

Please note: We reserve the right to change the terms of this offer (including the contents of the Welcome Pack) at any time but we offer a 14 day no-quibble money-back guarantee. We do not sell directly to children - all communications (except the Welcome Pack) will be via parents/guardians. After 31/12/96 please call to check that the price is still valid. Please allow 28 days for delivery. Promoter: Robell Media Promotions Limited, registered in England number 2852153.

MR. BUSY

by Roger Hargreaves

WORLD INTERNATIONAL

MANCHESTER

There has never been anybody quite like Mr Busy.

He could do things ten times as fast as ever you or I could.

For instance, if he was reading this book, he'd have finished it by now.

He lived in a very busy-looking house which he'd built himself.

As you can see.

It had lots of doors and windows, and do you know what it was called?

Weekend Cottage!

Do you know why?

Because that's how long it took him to build it!

One fine summer morning, Mr Busy was up and about bright and early at 6 o'clock.

He jumped out of bed and had a bath, and cleaned his teeth, and cooked his breakfast, and ate his breakfast, and read the paper, and washed up, and made his bed, and cleaned the house from top to bottom.

By which time it was 7 o'clock.

Busy Mr Busy!

Now, next door to Mr Busy lived someone who wasn't quite such a busy person.

In fact, a very unbusy person.

Mr Slow!

If he was reading this book he'd . . . read . . . it . . . like . . . this!

He'd still be on the first page!

And that same fine summer morning, at five past seven, when Mr Busy knocked at his door, Mr Slow was fast asleep in bed.

He'd gone to bed for an afternoon nap the day before, and somehow hadn't woken up until he heard Mr Busy knocking at his door.

"Who's . . . that . . . knocking . . . at . . . my . . . door?" he called downstairs.

"Good morning," cried Mr Busy. "Can I come in?"

And, without waiting for an answer, he went inside.

"Where are you?" he called.

"Up . . . stairs," came the slow reply.

So Mr Busy went upstairs, two at a time.

"Good heavens!" he said. "You're still in bed!"

And he made Mr Slow get up.

And he made his bed for him, and cooked his breakfast for him, and cleaned his house for him.

Poor Mr Slow.

He hated to be rushed and fussed.

"Right," said Mr Busy briskly. "It's a fine day. Let's go for a picnic."

Mr Slow pulled a face.

"I . . . don't . . . like . . . picnics," he complained.

"Nonsense," replied Mr Busy, and busied himself around Mr Slow's kitchen making up a picnic for the two of them.

It took him a minute and a half.

"Right," he cried when he'd finished. "Off we go!"

And he bustled Mr Slow out of his front door, and off they set.

As you can imagine, Mr Busy walks extremely quickly.

And, as you can imagine, Mr Slow doesn't.

So, by the time Mr Busy had walked a mile, do you know how far Mr Slow had walked?

To his own garden gate!

Mr Busy hurried back.

"Come on," he cried impatiently. "Hurry up!"

"Hurry . . . up?" replied Mr Slow.

"Im . . . poss . . . i . . . ble!"

"Oh, all right," said Mr Busy. "We'll have a picnic in your garden."

"Wait a minute, though," he added. "The grass needs cutting."

And he rushed back to Weekend Cottage and rushed back again with his lawnmower, and rushed up and down cutting Mr Slow's lawn.

It took him two and a half minutes!

It would have taken him two minutes, but he had to mow around Mr Slow who couldn't get out of the way in time.

"Right," cried Mr Busy. "Picnic time!"

And together on that fine summer day they had a fine picnic.

Well, actually, Mr Busy had a finer picnic than Mr Slow because he ate more quickly and had most of the food.

Mr Busy stretched out on the grass.

"That was fun," he said. "I like picnics!"

"You . . . do! . . . I . . . don't," said Mr Slow.

"Tell you what," went on Mr Busy, ignoring him. "Tomorrow we'll go on a proper picnic, out in the country."

Mr Slow pulled a face.

"And," went on Mr Busy, "in order to do that and get you out into the country, I'll have to call for you earlier than I did this morning."

Mr Slow pulled another face.

"See you tomorrow then," said Mr Busy, and went home and cleaned his house from bottom to top.

The following morning, Mr Busy jumped out of bed at 5 o'clock and had a bath and cleaned his teeth, and cooked his breakfast, and ate his breakfast, and read the paper, and washed up, and made his bed, and cleaned the house from top to bottom.

By which time it was 6 o'clock.

He went and knocked on Mr Slow's front door.

"Come on! Come on!" he cried. "Time to be up and about! Picnic day!"

No reply.

"Come on!" cried Mr Busy again.

No reply.

Mr Busy went inside.

And went upstairs, three at a time, and into Mr Slow's bedroom, expecting to find him in bed.

But he wasn't.

And he wasn't anywhere upstairs.

And he wasn't anywhere downstairs.

"Bother," said Mr Busy. "I wonder where he's got to?"

Where Mr Slow had got to was under his bed.

Hiding!

He didn't want to go on any picnic.

Not he.

"Bother," said Mr Busy again. "That means I'll have to go on a picnic on my own!"

Under his bed, Mr Slow smiled a slow smile.

"What . . . a . . . good . . . idea," he said.

And went to sleep.

Snoring very slowly.